Sarah and the People of Sand River

To my great-grandparents,
William Herbert Bristow and
Gudrun Fridrikka Gottskalksdottir — W D V

To my friends Steve, Stephanie and Brock,
and especially Adrienne, who brought
Sarah to life — I W

The artist wishes to thank Magnus Einarsson, Curator, North European Programme, Canadian Centre for Folk Culture Studies, Canadian Museum of Civilization, Ottawa.

Groundwood Books /Douglas & McIntyre Ltd.
585 Bloor Street West
Toronto, Ontario M6G 1K5

Distributed in the United States by
Publishers Group West
4065 Hollis Street
Emeryville, CA 94608

The publisher gratefully acknowledges the assistance of the Canada Council and the Ontario Arts Council.

Canadian Cataloguing in Publication Data

Valgardson, W.D.
 Sarah and the people of Sand River

ISBN 0-88899-255-6

1. Picture books for children. I. Wallace, Ian, 1950-
II. Title
PS8593.A53S37 1996   jC813'.54   C96-930017-4
PZ7.V35Sa 1996

The illustrations are done in pencil, watercolors and gouache
Book design by Michael Solomon
Printed in Hong Kong by
Everbest Printing Co. Ltd.

Sarah and the People of Sand River

By W. D. VALGARDSON
Pictures by IAN WALLACE

A GROUNDWOOD BOOK

DOUGLAS & McINTYRE   VANCOUVER / TORONTO / BUFFALO

One

When Sarah was twelve her father told her that she would have to leave home. She did not understand at first. She thought she had done something wrong. She thought her father was angry with her. But he said no, he was not angry. She thought maybe he did not love her anymore, but he said he loved her as much as ever. The next day, after breakfast, he said she would have to move to the city.

"Baldur will hate the city," she said. Baldur was her dog. "He's lived here all his life. Like me."

"Baldur's not going," her father said.

"Who will look after him?" she asked. "He can't stay here by himself."

"I'll look after him," her father said. "We're good friends, he and I."

"I can't go by myself," Sarah said. "I've never been to the city. I don't know anybody. What will I do all day?"

"Go to school," her father said. "And learn to speak English instead of Icelandic."

"And who will take care of Hjortur?" she demanded. Hjortur was their horse. He hauled wood for their stove and pulled the sleigh when they went ice fishing in winter. He was the strongest horse on the whole lake. Sometimes Sarah rode on his back.

"I'll take care of Hjortur," her father answered.

"And who will work with you?" Although Sarah was only twelve, she knew how to set and lift nets. "I'm as strong as any boy. I can chisel ice. Besides, who will you talk to? Loki?" Loki was a raven her father had rescued. She had taught him to say "Loki" and "Baldur" and "hello."

"It won't be easy," her father said, and he went out to mend his nets.

Sarah could not imagine leaving Frog Bay. Her grandparents had come here from Iceland. They had cleared two acres by hand. They had used the spruce logs to build a cabin. Her father had been born here. She had been born here. She knew where the moose fed, where the bears slept in winter, and where to find grass snakes in spring.

This was no ordinary place. Sarah's family had given it a history. Her grandparents never locked their door to anyone. Travel on Lake Winnipeg was dangerous, and people arrived unexpectedly at all hours of the day and night. They knew they could always warm themselves at the fire, sleep on the floor and share whatever food there was. From the beginning the Cree from Sand River often stopped here because the camp was right across from their village on the east side of the lake.

Ever since she could remember, Sarah had heard her father tell the story of how there were no fish during her grandparents' first year at Frog Bay, and coming from a country where there were no wild animals, her grandfather knew little about hunting.

When people talked about that year, they called it the Hunger Year. The Cree saw that Sarah's grandparents had only a little flour to eat. They brought moose meat and smoked fish and dried berries. Helgi and Fjola, Sarah's grandparents, often knew that the Cree had passed by during the night, because when they got up in the morning there would be food or clothing on the table. Without the gifts from the people of Sand River, they would never have survived the Hunger Year.

The next spring a family from Sand River arrived by canoe. Sarah's grandfather found the canoe rocking in the shallows. He knew, as soon as he saw them, that the whole family had smallpox. The man who worked for him said they should push the canoe back into the lake and let it take its ill luck elsewhere. Sarah's grandfather refused. He quoted a verse from "Havamal," an old Icelandic poem.

"Cattle die and kinsmen die. And so one dies oneself. One thing I know never dies. The fame of a dead man's deeds."

Her grandfather had meant that doing what was right was more important than anything else.

The hired man was too afraid to help, so Sarah's grandfather and grandmother carried the man and woman and two children ashore. They took care of them as best they could, but there was no medicine for smallpox and the family died. They buried them to one side of the camp and piled the graves with stones. Before the woman died, she took a pendant of Mary and the Christ child from around her neck and gave it to Sarah's grandmother. It was made of brightly colored beads stitched on deer hide.

"It is all I have," the woman said. "But always wear it. If any of my people see it, they will know you are a friend."

Sarah had heard this story many times. Her father showed her where the canoe had drifted ashore. There was a large stone there where crayfish could always be found. The graves were on the edge of the bush close to the water, because before he died the man had asked to be buried where he could see the lake. Sarah was not afraid of the graves. They were the graves of friends. Sometimes she collected flowers to put on them.

Sarah's mother was not buried at the camp. She became sick when Sarah was six. Sarah and her father took her mother south to see a doctor. Sarah did not remember much about it except for her mother lying in the boat wrapped in a blanket. She remembered coming back without her mother and feeling very lonely. Then there had been a letter saying that her mother had died. Someone sent the pendant to her father. He gave the pendant to Sarah. She would, she promised herself, always wear it. As long as she did, it would be a little like having her grandmother and mother with her.

When Sarah's father came in from mending his nets, he said, "I wrote to Winnipeg to find you a place to stay. A Mrs. Simpson is going to take care of you."

"I could stay with someone Icelandic," Sarah protested.

"No," he replied. "If you do that, you'll just keep speaking Icelandic. You won't learn to speak English or make English friends. We're in Canada now."

"I can learn English from books," she said. "I've learned Icelandic from books."

"You also need to learn to be a lady. You can't spend all your time snaring rabbits and hunting ducks. You have to meet other girls your own age."

Girls her own age. That intrigued Sarah. She seldom got to meet anyone her own age. She wondered what that would be like. What would they talk about? She didn't think they would know how to catch and clean fish.

Sarah had never been to a city. The idea frightened her but it also excited her. Her father described the roads and all the houses, but she could not really imagine it.

She wondered what Mrs. Simpson would be like. She hoped she would be something like her mother. Her mother had always combed her long blonde hair for her and braided it. Sarah wondered if Mrs. Simpson would comb her hair. Not that she needed anyone to do it since she was all grown up, but somehow, when she felt lonely or sad, she wished her mother was there to comb her hair and talk to her.

When it came time to leave, Sarah begged to take Baldur, but her father said Baldur could never live in the city. Besides, he needed him to keep the wolves away.

"You won't need Baldur to guide you in the city." To cheer her up, he said, "Mrs. Simpson has a daughter. She's two years younger than you. It will be like having a sister. You've often said you wished you had a sister."

Two

It was a long journey. It took Sarah and her father all day to reach Mikley, the big island where a colony of Icelanders had settled. They stayed overnight at one of the houses. The housewife gave Sarah five lumps of sugar with her breakfast coffee. She explained how girls were supposed to sit properly in a chair with their ankles crossed. Sarah explained to her how to skin a squirrel so she could make a fringe for her mittens.

Sarah and her father boarded a freight boat and traveled on it to the south end of Lake Winnipeg, then up the river to Selkirk. Sarah was amazed to see the houses along the river. Some were made of wood like her own house, but some were made of stone.

At Selkirk they boarded a train, and all her father's descriptions did not prepare her for the noise of the whistle or the motion. There were more people on the train than she had seen in her entire life. And they were always talking. At home it was so quiet that she could hear a cricket move in the grass or a leaf fall on the snow.

When they got off the train in Winnipeg, they put Sarah's box onto a cart and rode to Mrs. Simpson's. Her house was made of wood and was two stories high. There were four lines of clothes in the backyard.

Mrs. Simpson was a large, square woman with a loud voice and big red arms that she crossed in front of her. Her daughter, Eugenie, sounded and looked like her mother.

"She looks healthy enough," Mrs. Simpson said when she saw Sarah. "She'll have to help around the house."

"Of course," her father said. "She's a hard worker."

Although Sarah cried when her father got up to leave, he could not stay. He had to get back to take care of Hjortur and Baldur and Loki.

For the first week Mrs. Simpson treated Sarah well. But once she was certain that Sarah's father was not going to come back suddenly, she began to be mean to her. Sarah's father was paying for her room and board. He also gave Mrs. Simpson some money for Sarah to buy things for herself. Mrs. Simpson kept all the money and used it to buy treats and clothes for Eugenie. If Sarah was using something and Eugenie wanted it, Mrs. Simpson made Sarah give it to her. Sometimes she beat Sarah on the arms and shoulders with a wooden spoon.

At the end of the second week, Mrs. Simpson put Sarah to work. It became her job to wash the dishes, to set the table, to wash the floors, to get the water and the wood.

Mrs. Simpson had promised to send Sarah to school but she did not. She kept Sarah at home, saying that until she learned to speak more English, there was no point in her going to school.

Sarah was dreadfully lonely. There were no children to play with at Frog Bay, but there were baby rabbits in the spring and for a time she had a bear cub that had lost its mother. She and Baldur explored the bush and lake shore. She told Mrs. Simpson how Loki would sometimes come into the cabin when the door was open and sit on the back of a chair until he got a piece of bread.

"How dreadful," Mrs. Simpson said. "A dirty animal in the house." She told Sarah to get busy and quit wasting time.

Shortly after that a raven appeared. He sat on the house's peak. On the coldest days he huddled close to the chimney. Mrs. Simpson threw sticks at the bird, saying it was bad luck. The raven flew away, then returned.

"Loki?" Sarah called. But he didn't come and sit on her shoulder or say "Baldur" or "hello" so she doubted he was Loki. Still, she was glad to see the raven. Her father had told her that the day she was born, a raven perched on the roof of their cabin. A Cree midwife was helping with the birth, and she said the bird had chosen the child.

One of Sarah's jobs was to bring in wood for the fire. The wood was stacked in a long pile in the backyard. During the fall fetching wood was not a difficult task, but once the winter started, the pile was covered in snow and hoarfrost. When Sarah touched the frost, her hands burned. As she worked, the raven gave his clunking cry. She dropped the wood and with tears in her eyes scolded, "If you chose me, why don't you help me? Can't you see how cold my hands are?"

The raven fell silent. Sarah went back to knocking wood free from the pile. She heard a swish of wings and when she looked up, the raven was gone.

Suddenly a woman appeared from behind the woodpile. She had long dark hair and was wrapped from head to foot in a thick cloak made from a Hudson Bay blanket. She held out a pair of deerskin mittens. The backs were finely decorated with brightly colored beads, and the cuffs were trimmed with wolf fur.

As soon as Sarah put the mittens on, her hands were no

longer cold. When she looked up, the woman was gone. Sarah ran to the end of the woodpile, but all she saw was a brief flash of red. She would have followed, but just then Mrs. Simpson came to the back door and yelled, "Where's my wood? What's taking you so long?" Quickly Sarah began to pull the wood free. She carried six armloads to the back porch, then hid the mittens in the woodpile where they would not be found.

The reason there were so many clotheslines was because
Mrs. Simpson was a laundress. At the end of the first month
she gave Sarah a sled and told her to pick up and deliver laundry. When Sarah asked why Eugenie could not do it, Mrs.
Simpson said Eugenie had to practice her piano and do her
homework. Sarah, she said, did not need to learn music or
other things because she was just going to live in the bush like
her father.

Sarah picked up and delivered laundry in snow that was
nearly up to her knees. She had no winter boots, only thin
leather shoes. Her feet got so cold that when she returned to
Mrs. Simpson's house, she cried when her feet started to thaw.
Wherever she went, the raven flapped along behind her but he
never came close and never spoke.

One bitterly cold day a dark-haired man came out of an alleyway and grabbed Sarah's arm. Sarah was afraid, but his voice was quiet and gentle. He held his finger to his lips, then handed her a pair of deerskin moccasins.

Sarah put her shoes in her pockets and put on the moccasins. They were thin and light and lined with fur and felt. After she put them on, her feet were no longer cold. When she got home, she hid them beside her mittens in the woodpile.

One day as she was delivering a bundle of clothes, Sarah was lonelier than usual. The raven was following her, flitting from rooftop to rooftop. "I'm so unhappy," she shouted at him. "What good is it having a raven for a friend? Stop following me."

After she delivered the clothes, she noticed that the raven was nowhere to be seen. There was no raven the next morning when she pulled water on a sled, nor that afternoon when she took out the slop pail. Mrs. Simpson noticed. "Some cat got it," she said happily.

Normally Sarah wore her pendant over her shawl. But the next morning she was so worried about the raven that she left her pendant lying on her dresser. Eugenie saw it and put it on. Sarah tried to take it back but Mrs. Simpson rained down blows on her shoulders and head with her wooden spoon.

"It's just a cheap trinket," Mrs. Simpson said. "She won't hurt it."

"It was my mother's," Sarah cried.

"She'll give it back to you later," Mrs. Simpson replied.

But Eugenie did not give it back. She lost it.

Sarah was frantic. She searched everywhere. "What am I going to do?" she asked herself. But the pendant was nowhere to be found.

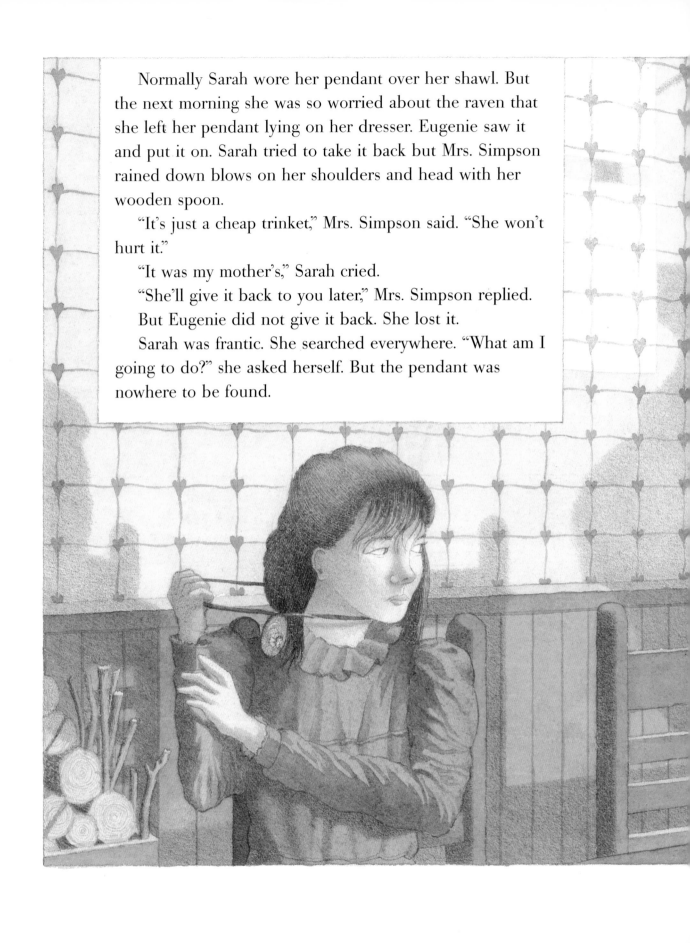

The next day she cleared snow from the woodpile and put out a piece of fat and some porridge. "I'm sorry," she said out loud to the sky. "I wish you'd come back. A raven is a good friend to have."

There was no raven that day, or the next. Each day Sarah added something to the pile and said she was sorry.

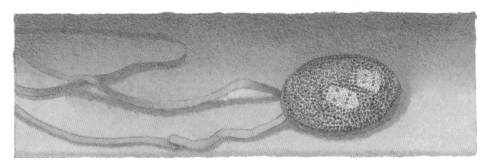

As she was getting ready to deliver laundry the third day, she heard the dry, wooden clunking of a raven. She ran out of the house. She knew that if her pendant was outside, the raven would find it. Loki always was finding shiny things. She often traded him a piece of smoked fish or bacon for the bright objects he brought.

She had a crust of bread in her pocket. She held it out. The raven tipped his head to one side, then the other. It was then that Sarah saw something bright in his beak. Something that gleamed in the winter sunlight.

It might, she told herself, just be a piece of colored cloth. When she tried to get close, the raven flew onto the roof. She took the ladder from beside the woodpile and put it against the house. She climbed up to get a better look at the treasure in the raven's beak.

Just then the door banged and Mrs. Simpson yelled, "Sarah! What's keeping you?"

The raven was startled. He hopped backward and let go of the shiny object which slid down the roof into the eaves. Sarah scampered down the ladder and hurried into the house with the wood.

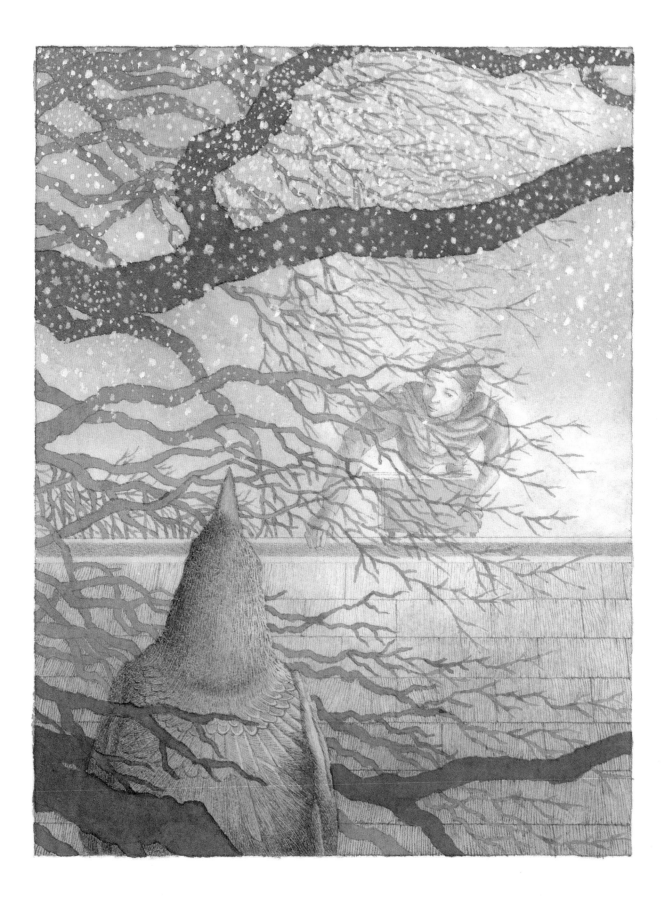

Later, when Mrs. Simpson was busy, Sarah slipped outside and searched the eaves. They were full of snow but she scraped it away. There was the pendant. The raven was watching her from the chimney.

"I'm sorry," she said. "I shouldn't have said what I said. You don't know how important a friend is until he's not there anymore."

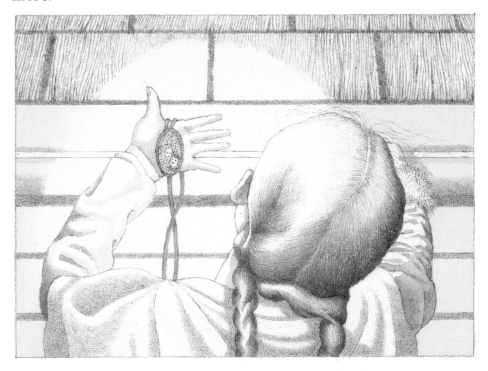

That night Sarah went to sleep with the pendant around her neck. Rather than risk Eugenie taking any of her other small belongings, she searched around the room and found that the ball on the iron bedpost could be unscrewed. The tube was hollow. She stuffed a rag inside so the tube was nearly full, then lay her eagle's feather and her bear's tooth on the rag and screwed back the ball.

Before she went downstairs to set the table, she said to herself, "I've got to count my blessings. A stranger has given me warm mittens. Another has given me warm moccasins. Now the raven has brought back my pendant."

Three

As the winter deepened, the weather grew colder and sharper, so that Sarah coughed when she went outside, and her chest ached. Her shawl could not keep out the cold. She ran to keep warm as she delivered the clothes, and she beat her arms against her sides as she waited at people's doors. The raven never abandoned her. And she never forgot to save a scrap from her meal for him.

After the second week of bitterly cold weather, the woman in the red blanket cloak stopped her at a street corner. She reached out and touched the pendant that Sarah wore over her

shawl. Then she reached into a bundle she was carrying and took out a jacket. It was made of soft leather. It had a fringe and smelled of smoke. It was decorated with flowers made from beads.

The woman handed the jacket to Sarah.

Quickly Sarah caught her hand. "Who are you? You and the man who brought me my moccasins."

The woman said something soft and flowing, but Sarah could not understand it. "What?" she asked. "Tell me again."

The woman said the same thing again. All the way back to Mrs. Simpson's, Sarah repeated the phrases to herself. She hid the jacket in the woodpile with her moccasins and mittens. When she was in her room, she wrote down the words just as the woman had said them.

For the next month Sarah ran errands, even when the air was so cold that there were sun dogs in the sky. When she delivered laundry some of the regular customers began to give her money for herself. She put the money into the bedpost. She was starting to make a plan.

She thought about the trip to the city with her father. They had left on his boat and traveled all day. They had stayed at Mikley. They had taken a large boat to another town. There they had taken a train.

Sarah was sure she could retrace her steps. Take the train, then the big boat, then get a ride with someone traveling north on the lake.

One day, after dropping off her first load of laundry, Sarah went to the train station. She had learned the names of the streets and where things were in the weeks and months of delivering laundry. The station no longer seemed so big and noisy. There were many doors and many people rushing about, but she was used to the city now. She realized to her dismay that there was more than one train. The next day she asked one of her customers how she would take a train ride and how much a ticket would cost.

"A train ride," the woman said, amused. "And where would you be going on a train?"

"To see my father."

"And where is he?"

"New Iceland," Sarah said.

Everyone knew about the settlement called New Iceland. Sarah knew that if she got there, there would be many people who could speak Icelandic. She was sure that if she could find the housewife who had given her the sugar lumps, she would help her find her father.

"Are you homesick?" the woman asked. Sarah nodded. Sick for home. Sick for Baldur. Sick for her father.

The woman put her arm around Sarah. She gave her a cookie with raisins in it and a cup of tea with milk. She offered to give Sarah a warm sweater. When Sarah took off her jacket to put on the sweater, the woman saw the bruises on her arms. She told Sarah that to get to New Iceland, she first had to take the train to Selkirk. She wrote "Selkirk" on a piece of paper for her.

"Selkirk," was all Sarah could think about on her way back to Mrs. Simpson's. Soon she would have enough money saved for a train ticket.

Back at the house Mrs. Simpson was sitting at the kitchen table with a wooden spoon in her hand. Her face was bright red.

"You're going to run away, are you? You're going to take a train ride? You little wretch. I've fed you and given you a home and you repay me by losing me a customer."

Mrs. Simpson grabbed Sarah by the hair and dragged her to the bedroom and tied her to the bed by one ankle. "You'll stay there until you get rid of any ideas of running anywhere."

As Sarah lay on the bed crying, Eugenie came in. She opened her hand and showed Sarah some coins. Sarah sat up and unscrewed the ball on the bedpost. The money was gone.

Mrs. Simpson came to the door. "Stealing from me, my girl. I could have you put in jail. You mind your p's and q's or I'll have the police on you."

Four

That night Sarah cried herself to sleep. She dreamed of the raven. He was flying ahead of her, leading her home.

For the next week Mrs. Simpson kept a close watch over Sarah. But on Sunday Mrs. Simpson and Eugenie went to church. There was a blizzard. Snow was whirling in the air. "You won't be going anywhere in this," Mrs. Simpson said.

As soon as they were gone, Sarah left the house. She went straight to the woodpile for her warm clothes.

At the train station she asked which track led to Selkirk. A man pointed it out to her. Snow was already drifting over the tracks. Sarah could not see far but she knew the tracks would lead her to where she wanted to go. The raven flew ahead of her, then behind her, appearing and disappearing in the whirling snow.

Gradually the snow became so deep that Sarah could barely push her way forward. The cold began to seep through her moccasins and mittens. Even her warm coat couldn't keep it away. She was about to lie down and rest, when the woman in the red coat appeared and crooked her finger. Sarah started forward. The woman stayed just ahead of her, beckoning.

Sarah did not make it to Selkirk. She was stumbling along the tracks when a young boy saw her. He was pulling a sled with food for his family. He gently helped her onto his sled, then Sarah fainted. She was delirious for two days and spoke nothing but Icelandic. When she woke up on the third day, an Icelander had come from Selkirk to speak to her.

He asked her how she had walked in a blizzard from Winnipeg and survived. Loki, she said, had led the way. They thought she was delirious again but the boy who found her said there had been a raven. That was what had attracted his attention. A raven fluttering above a snowdrift.

"I was lost," Sarah explained, "but someone came and showed me the way. Where are my mittens and moccasins and jacket? I'll need them to continue my journey."

"There were no such clothes when I found her," the boy said. "She had only a shawl and shoes."

They sent for her father. He came right away. He had sent her letters but had only received brief notes from Mrs. Simpson saying that Sarah was doing fine and was too busy to write.

Sarah told her father about the man and woman who had brought her clothes. She showed him the scrap of paper on which she had written what the woman had said. Her father said it sounded Cree. He went to check with friends, and when he came back he brought a Cree woman with him. Sarah repeated the words.

The Cree woman looked puzzled. Then she said, "Those words mean 'We are the people of Sand River.' But no one has lived at Sand River for more than forty years. Not since the smallpox epidemic. They all died. And the village was burned."

Five

My great-grandmother told me this story. She was the girl, Sarah. And the boy who found her eventually became her husband and moved to New Iceland and became one of us. When she was very old, my great-grandmother made my father take her by car and then by boat back to where her father's fish camp had been. She took with her a headstone. Carved on one side in Cree and on the other in Icelandic were the words THE PEOPLE OF SAND RIVER.

My father and great-grandmother found the old cabin with its roof caved in. They found the graves of the Cree family that had died of smallpox. The clearing was overgrown with grass and moose maple. They cut the grass and set the stone at the head of the graves so the people of Sand River would not be forgotten.

HISTORICAL NOTE

In 1875, large volcanic eruptions destroyed many farms and hayfields on the island of Iceland. Many Icelanders were starving, and they started emigrating to Canada. They tried settling in a number of places but finally decided to create a colony called New Iceland, a large tract of land on the western shore of Lake Winnipeg.

The first group of 235 settlers did not arrive in Manitoba until mid October. The captain who was to tow the Icelanders' barges to the colony was afraid of the lake freezing, so he cut them loose before they reached their planned destination. The barges drifted ashore at a spot that was so unsuitable for settlement that thirty-five people died during the first winter. Despite the difficult conditions, however, the Icelanders stayed on and created the community of Gimli.

The following year, twelve hundred settlers joined the first group. Shortly after they arrived, a smallpox epidemic hit the community. During the winter, more than one hundred people died, and the disease spread to the native people who also lived in the area.

The native people and the Icelanders shared other difficulties, too. Both peoples suffered discrimination from the Europeans, French and English who had settled in southern Manitoba.

Sarah's story is made up, but her experiences are based on true events and people.

—WDV

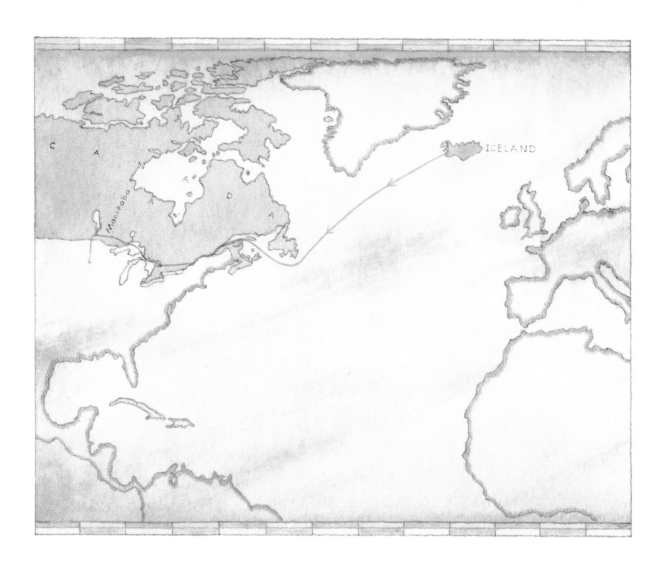

ICELAND

DOMINION LAND OFFICE,
OTTAWA,
31ST DECEMBER 1878.

Lindsay Russell

SURVEYOR GENERAL

SAND
RIVER

W I N N I

L A K E

MIKLEY

FROG
BAY

M A N I